Meet the Kreeps

The New
Step-Mummy

Meet the Kreeps

The New Step-Mummy

by Kiki Thorpe

Scholastic Inc.

New York • Toronto • London • Auckland • Sydney
Mexico City • New Delhi • Hong Kong • Buenos Aires

No part of this publication may be reproduced, stored in
a retrieval system, or transmitted in any form or by any
means, electronic, mechanical, photocopying, recording,
or otherwise, without written permission of the publisher.
For information regarding permission, write to
Scholastic Inc., Attention: Permissions Department,
557 Broadway, New York, NY 10012.

ISBN-13: 978-0-545-06562-7
ISBN-10: 0-545-06562-3

Copyright © 2008 by Kiki Thorpe.
All rights reserved. Published by Scholastic Inc.
SCHOLASTIC, APPLE PAPERBACKS, and associated
logos are trademarks and/or registered trademarks of
Scholastic Inc.

12 11 10 9 8 7 6 5 4 3 2 1   8 9 10 11 12 13/0

Printed in the U.S.A.
First printing, September 2008

For my mummy

❋ Chapter 1 ❋

Polly Winkler sat at the kitchen table, trying to eat her breakfast. It was a bright summer morning. Out the window, she could see sprinklers watering her neighbor's front lawn and birds fluttering around the trees. *Outside, it seems like a normal day*, Polly thought. But inside the Winklers' house, things were anything *but* normal.

"No, no, no!" her father, Wally Winkler, exclaimed into the phone, a cup of coffee sloshing in one hand. "We ordered steak for two dozen — *steak,* not *snake*! Where on earth did you get that idea?"

Polly scooped a spooonful of cornflakes into her mouth and grimly chewed. It was hard to enjoy her breakfast amid all the commotion. Her sister, Joy, was also shouting. Joy was a cheerleader, and her voice really carried.

"Did you call the florist, Dad?" she cried. "What about the balloons? You can't have a wedding without balloons!"

Finally, Polly put down her spoon. *It's official*, she thought. *My family has gone completely bonkers.* And Polly was sure that her "famous imagination" wasn't to blame this time.

In just two days, Dr. Winkler was getting married, and it seemed to Polly like her family had gone wedding-crazy. The only person who wasn't in a frenzy was Polly's brother, Petey. He was calmly sitting at the breakfast table, looking at the dictionary.

Polly nudged him with her toe. "It's rude to read at the table, Petey," she reminded him.

Petey looked up, annoyed. "Well, it's rude to touch people with your feet," he said. "Besides, I'm not reading. I'm memorizing."

"The *dictionary*?" asked Polly.

"It's the best place to find spelling words," he replied. Petey was the Endsville Elementary spelling bee champion, a fact that he often liked to bring up.

"But it's summertime," Polly pointed out. "Nobody memorizes stuff in the summer."

"I don't want to lose my competitive edge," Petey said with a shrug. He went back to studying.

Polly sighed. *Petey hasn't gone wedding crazy*, she thought. *He's just plain old crazy.*

Just then, a knock came at their back door. Polly got up to answer it. Veronica Kreep, Polly's soon-to-be stepmother, was standing there, along with her three children — Vincent, Damon, and Esmerelda.

"Veronica!" Dr. Winkler cried when he saw her. He hung up the phone and hurried over to kiss her pale cheek.

"I tried to call before we came," Veronica said apologetically. "But the line has been busy all morning."

"I've been on the phone making sure everything is set for the wedding," Dr. Winkler explained. "You wouldn't believe how the caterer mixed up our order!"

"How odd," said Veronica, frowning. "I spoke with them just yesterday, and everything seemed fine."

"Well, don't worry," Dr. Winkler said,

squeezing her hand. "I got it all straightened out." Watching them, Polly wondered,
not for the first time, how her father and
Veronica had ever fallen in love. Veronica
was not at all like Polly's goofy, dentist dad.
In fact she wasn't like anyone Polly had ever
met. Instead of jeans and sneakers, Veronica
wore long, black dresses and pointy boots.
Instead of flowers, she grew carnivorous
plants. And when she cleaned, Veronica
didn't dust away the spiderwebs — she
dusted *around* them.

Veronica's kids were as strange as she
was. Vincent, the oldest, was tall and pale.
He always wore a black hooded sweatshirt,
and he almost never smiled. Damon, his
younger brother, smiled all the time. But it
was a crafty smile, like he was up to something. Damon's hair stuck straight up on
his head, and he often wore a lab coat and
safety goggles. Esmerelda, the youngest,

had a thin, white face, pigtails, and huge, green eyes. Her favorite pet was a tarantula named Bubbles. Polly couldn't imagine having them as her brothers and sister any more than she could imagine having Veronica as a mother.

The problem was, the rest of her family didn't seem to think there was anything weird about the Kreeps. When Polly pointed out that the Kreeps' car looked like a hearse, her dad said, "Don't be silly, Polly." When she mentioned that she'd seen bats flying around the Kreeps' house, her sister told her she was imagining things. Polly was known for having a vivid imagination. But she didn't think she was imagining that there was something truly strange about the Kreeps.

"What are you all doing out so early?" Dr. Winkler asked Veronica now.

"We're on our way back from the airport," she replied. "We were picking up Uncle Vlad."

"Uncle Vlad?" Dr. Winkler scratched his head. "I don't remember you mentioning him."

"Of course I did, darling," Veronica said. "He's on the Transylvanian side of the family. He flew in on the red-eye last night."

"Well, why don't you bring him in?" asked Dr. Winkler. "I'd love to meet him."

"He's asleep in the car," Veronica said with a little frown. "And I'd rather not wake him up. He's not much of a morning person."

"You can say that again," Vincent remarked with a snort.

"Anyway," said Veronica, "I just wanted to stop by and let the girls know that the bridesmaid dresses are ready. They can come over and try them on this afternoon."

"Awesome!" cried Joy, throwing her arms around Veronica. "I'm so excited for the wedding!"

"Er, I'm glad, dear." Veronica gasped. Her eyes bugged a little from Joy's tight squeeze.

Dr. Winkler checked his watch. "I'd better get going," he said. "I've got a lot to do today."

"We have to be going, too," Veronica said. "We'll see you girls this afternoon."

The Kreeps filed out. But at the door, Veronica turned. "You know," she said, "maybe I should check in with the caterer again. Just to make sure they have our order right."

"Good idea," said Dr. Winkler, who was already on the phone. He waved good-bye.

"After all," Veronica said to no one in particular, "a party just isn't a party without roasted rattlesnake."

She gave Polly a wink, then turned and headed out the door.

Polly stared after her. *Rattlesnake?* she thought. *This wedding is getting crazier by the minute!*

❊ Chapter 2 ❊

I'm sure that can't be right," said Joy after the Kreeps had left.

"I'm telling you, Veronica said we're having rattlesnake for dinner," Polly said. She turned to her brother. "You heard her, didn't you, Petey?"

Petey didn't answer. Polly poked him.

"Huh?" said Petey, looking up from the dictionary.

"Never mind," Polly said with a sigh.

Joy picked up a pile of breakfast dishes and carried them to the sink. "You probably just didn't hear her right, Polly.

You have such a wild imagination," she said.

"I did *not* imagine it," Polly snapped. She hated it when Joy acted like a know-it-all big sister. But she knew it was pointless to keep arguing.

Polly left her brother and sister in the kitchen and went outside. She sat down on the front porch with her chin in her hands. Across the street, she could see Vincent and Damon in the driveway of the Kreeps' spooky old mansion. They were unloading a wooden box from the back of the Kreeps' hearse-like black station wagon.

Polly looked closer. The box was long, with handles on the sides. It looked almost like —

"A coffin!" Polly whispered.

Polly's heart started to beat faster. The Kreeps said they had gone to the airport to pick up their uncle. *Their uncle from Transylvania!* Polly thought. *Vampires come from Transylvania. And they also sleep in coffins!*

Is Uncle Vlad a vampire? she wondered with a gulp.

Polly had to tell someone. Someone who would listen. She hopped off the porch, grabbed her bike, and headed over to her friend Mike's house.

When she got there, she found Mike in the backyard kicking an old soccer ball around.

"They are so weird!" Polly exclaimed, throwing her bike down in the grass.

"Let me guess," said Mike. "You're talking about the Kreeps."

"You're never going to believe what we're having for dinner at the wedding," Polly told him.

"Bat eyes?" Mike joked. "Slime soup? Frog toes?"

"Worse," said Polly. "Rattlesnake."

Mike's brown eyes lit up. "Cool!"

"Are you crazy?" asked Polly. "It's not cool. It's gross!"

Mike shrugged. "It might not be so bad," he said. "I heard it tastes like chicken."

"But that's not all," Polly said. She lowered her voice and leaned in close to Mike. "The Kreeps went to pick up their uncle from the airport this morning. And they came back with a coffin!"

"How do you know it was a coffin?" asked Mike. "Maybe it was just their uncle's luggage."

"It looked like a coffin," Polly said. "It was a big, wooden box with handles on the sides."

"I still don't get it," Mike said. "What would their uncle be doing with a coffin?"

"I'll give you one clue," Polly said. "He's from *Transylvania*."

Mike's eyes widened. "You mean, you think he's a *vampire*?"

Polly nodded. "You see? Even their relatives are creepy. And now I'm going to be stuck with them, just because Dad wants to get married."

"You used to really want your dad to get married," Mike said. "Remember?"

A few months before, Polly had set out to find the perfect mom for her family. But it hadn't worked out the way she had planned. Instead, her dad had fallen in love with Veronica.

"I wanted him to marry a *normal* person," Polly said. "Not a witch with vampire relatives."

"Well, once your dad and Veronica get married, she won't be a witch anymore," said Mike.

"What do you mean?" Polly asked.

"Because she'll be your mummy!" Mike hooted.

Polly punched him on the arm. "It's not funny!"

"Sorry." Mike smirked. "But come on. You don't seriously think Veronica is a witch, do you?"

"She sure *looks* like a witch," said Polly.

"She's weird all right," Mike said. "But just because she's weird doesn't mean she's a witch."

"Maybe not," Polly said, plucking a piece of grass. "But I still think there's something really spooky about that family."

"So, what are you going to do?" asked Mike.

"Well, to start with, I'm going to tell my dad about the rattlesnake," she decided. "And about the coffin."

Mike shook his head. "Bad idea," he said.

"Why?" asked Polly.

"He'll think you're making it up," Mike told her.

Polly frowned. Mike was right. Her father would say she had imagined it, just like he always did.

Polly chewed her lip thoughtfully. Despite what everyone else said, she had a feeling the Kreeps weren't normal people. The problem was, she couldn't prove it.

Suddenly, she sat up straight, her eyes wide. "But what if I could?" she said.

Mike looked up from the ball. "Could what?" he asked.

"Prove the truth about them," Polly said. "If I find out that the Kreeps really are, well, *creeps*, then Dad will have to call off the wedding, right?"

"I guess so," said Mike, frowning. "But how are you going to do that?"

"I don't know yet," Polly said. "But I'll figure it out."

She hopped to her feet and grabbed her bike from the grass. She had to find out the truth about the Kreeps. And she had just two days to do it.

❊ Chapter 3 ❊

That afternoon, Polly stood in an unused bedroom in the Kreeps' mansion, staring at her reflection in a cracked and dusty mirror.

"We're wearing *black*?" she asked in disbelief.

"Do you like it?" Veronica asked. "I think it's such a festive color."

Polly frowned into the mirror. Her bridesmaid dress looked like a big, black sack with bell-shaped sleeves. *All I need is a pointy hat and a broom, and I'll be ready for Halloween!* she thought.

Joy, who was wearing an identical dress, flashed a cheerleader grin. "It was nice of you to make these dresses, Veronica," she said. "They're really, um . . . elegant."

"Maybe, if you're a witch," Polly muttered, casting a glance in Veronica's direction.

"I think they look nice," piped up Esme, who was watching them.

Joy gave her a brilliant smile. "Are you excited for the wedding, sweetie?" she asked.

Esme took one look at Joy and hissed like a cat.

Joy blinked in suprise. Both Polly and Joy stared at Esme.

Veronica didn't seem to notice her daughter's strange behavior. She was still studying the dresses. "No, something about them isn't quite right. Give them back to me. I'll work some magic before the wedding," she said.

"*Magic?*" Polly looked at her sharply.

"With a needle and thread," Veronica explained.

"Oh." Polly sighed. Ever since she and Joy had gotten to the Kreeps' house, Polly had been on the lookout for clues. The problem was, she wasn't quite sure what she was looking for.

"So, um, where is Uncle Vlad?" Polly asked as she wriggled out of the dress.

"Still sleeping," said Veronica. "He's had such a long trip. I'm afraid we were late to pick him up this morning. He waited for ages at baggage claim."

"Hmm," said Polly.

She put on her jeans and t-shirt, then slipped on her right sneaker. But as she pulled on the left one, she felt something squirm.

"There's something in my shoe!" she shrieked. She caught a glimpse of a scaly tail before it disappeared into the toe.

Veronica picked up the shoe and shook it. A small, green lizard fell out. It landed on the floor and scuttled underneath the bed.

"Just a lizard," Veronica said, handing the sneaker back.

"But what was it doing in my shoe?" Polly asked.

Just then, her eyes fell on Esme. She was watching Polly and giggling.

That brat! Polly thought. She gave Esme a fierce scowl. Esme grinned back at her.

Polly quickly tied her shoes and stood up. Out the window, she could see Vincent and Damon trimming the hedges in the Kreeps' backyard.

If Vincent and Damon are outside and Veronica and Esme are in here, then there's no one to catch me snooping, Polly thought. *Now is the perfect time to look around.*

She turned to Veronica and asked, "May I use the bathroom?"

"Of course, dear," said Veronica. "But use the one at the end of the hall. Damon is breeding salamanders in the toilet here."

Yuck, Polly thought with a shudder. "Be back in a minute," she said, heading for the door.

The upstairs hallway was long and narrow. There were several closed doors on either side. Where should she begin?

Polly yanked open the nearest door. She jumped as something landed at her feet.

Looking closer, Polly sighed with relief. It was just a pair of rubber boots. She'd found a closet.

Suddenly, she heard a noise behind her. She spun around. But no one was there.

Polly's eyes swept the hallway. It was empty. She could hear Joy and Veronica still talking in the bedroom.

She was about to try the next door, when she heard it again: a tiny giggle. She turned in time to see something dart through a doorway.

Polly frowned. "Quit spying on me, Esme," she said.

Esme stepped out of the room. "What are you doing?" she asked Polly. She fiddled with her necklace. It was made of gold beads and fit tightly around her neck, almost like a collar.

"I'm looking for the bathroom," Polly lied.

"The bathroom is there," Esme said, pointing to a door at the opposite end of the hall.

Polly gritted her teeth. She didn't really need to use the bathroom. But now Esme was watching. Polly trudged down the hallway to the bathroom and stepped inside.

The room was pretty ordinary, except for a large claw-foot bathtub. Polly sat down on the edge of it and tried to decide what to do. If she wanted to look around, she would have to get Esme out of the way first. And she didn't have much time.

Suddenly, she had an idea.

Polly went back into the hallway. "Esme, how would you like to play a game?" she asked.

"What kind of game?" Esme asked suspiciously.

"Hide-and-seek," Polly told her.

Esme grinned. "That's my favorite game!"

"Good," said Polly. "I'll be It. You hide, and I will find you."

"You'll never find me!" Esme cried, hopping up and down with delight.

"That depends. You'll have to find a good hiding spot," Polly told her. "And be quiet as a mouse."

Esme frowned. "Not quiet as a mouse. Quiet as a cat," she told Polly.

"All right, as quiet as a cat," Polly agreed. "I'll close my eyes and count to ten. Ready?" She put her hands over her eyes and began to count slowly. "One . . . two . . . three . . ."

Esme scurried past her. A second later, Polly heard a door creak. She peeked between her fingers. Esme was sneaking into the closet.

". . . eight . . . nine . . . ten! Ready or not, here I come!" Polly took her hands away from her eyes. "Where could Esme be?" she said loudly.

A muffled snicker came from the closet.

That should keep her busy for a few minutes, Polly thought.

There was no time to waste. She went quickly to the first door in the hallway and tried the knob. The door opened easily.

The room was very dark. As Polly felt for a light switch, she had a terrible thought. What if she found Uncle Vlad . . . and he wasn't in his coffin anymore!

Her heart pounded. At last her fingers touched a switch. She flipped it on.

Polly gasped. Dragons, demons, and goblins leered at her from every corner of the room, their faces twisted in evil grimaces. It took Polly a moment to realize that they were all masks decorating the walls of a bedroom.

"Creepy," Polly whispered. She walked through the room, looking at every one. She felt as if the masks were staring back at her.

Just then, the hairs on the back of Polly's neck stood up, as if she really *was* being watched. She spun around and saw a shadow dart behind a dresser.

Something was following her! Her heart pounding, Polly crept over to the dresser.

Just as she reached it, a little black cat sprang out from underneath.

Polly almost laughed. She'd been scared out of her wits by a kitten!

The cat hopped onto a couch. It regarded Polly with big, green eyes.

"I've seen you before," Polly said to the cat. Veronica and Esme had once brought the cat with them to the public library. It had gotten away and upset the librarian.

Polly had chased the cat all over, but it had disappeared before she could catch it.

Something glittered on the cat's neck. Polly looked closer. It was wearing a collar of golden beads.

"That looks like Esme's necklace," Polly murmured. She noticed how much the cat's eyes looked like Esme's eyes, too.

Suddenly, Polly had a funny feeling. *What if the cat is Esme?* she thought. It was such a crazy idea, she almost couldn't believe it.

But the more Polly thought about it, the more she was sure she was right. The time she had seen the cat at the library, it had appeared out of nowhere — at the same moment that Esme had *dis*appeared. If the cat really was Esme, it was just the proof Polly needed.

As if the cat knew what she was thinking, it turned and darted out of the room.

Polly sprinted after it. This was just like the time she'd chased the cat in the library. But this time Polly was quicker. She cornered the cat and scooped it up in her arms.

"Let's go look in the closet, kitty," Polly said.

The cat squirmed and scratched her. But Polly held it tightly. She walked toward the closet.

At the door, Polly paused. Would Esme still be inside? She took a deep breath and turned the knob.

"There you are!" Joy exclaimed, coming down the hall.

Polly was so startled she jumped. The cat wriggled out of her arms and darted away.

"Ready to go?" Joy asked brightly.

"I . . . but . . . the cat," Polly stuttered.

Joy looked confused. "What cat?"

"The cat that . . ." Polly threw open the

door of the closet and began to dig through the clothes and shoes.

"Polly, what are you doing?" Joy asked.

"I'm looking for Esme!" Polly said. "We were playing hide-and-seek, and —"

"But Esme's right here," Joy said.

Polly spun around. Esme was standing right behind her, watching Polly with her big, green eyes.

She gave Polly a devilish grin. "I win," she said.

⊰ Chapter 4 ⊱

Polly expected to find strange things in the Kreeps' mansion. But she was not prepared for the sight that met her when she and Joy walked into their own house.

"What the . . ." Polly cried.

The place was filled with hideous flowers — buckets and buckets of them, all black as tar. It looked like an entire greenhouse had died in the Winklers' living room.

Petey was lying on the couch with his nose stuck in the dictionary. "Petey, what's going on?!" Joy asked him.

"I'm up to the *B*s," Petey informed her.

"She means, what's with all these creepy flowers?" Polly asked.

"Oh, those." Petey shrugged. "The florist dropped off the flowers for the wedding."

"Well, don't you think it's weird that they're all *black*?" Polly asked.

"What's weird is that *bandanna* has three *N*s, but *banana* has only two," said Petey, going back to his book.

Polly sighed. *Petey is so wrapped up in his spelling, he wouldn't notice if a banana hit him in the head,* she thought.

"The florist must have made a mistake," said Joy, looking worried. "I hope Veronica's not too upset."

"I hope *Dad's* not too upset," said Polly. "Where is he, anyway?"

"He's in the kitchen," Petey told her. "Now will you all please stop talking? I'm trying to study."

Polly hurried into the kitchen. Her dad was sitting at the table, talking with a man she'd never seen before.

"Dad," said Polly, "did you know our living room is full of black tulips?"

"Calla lilies, actually," said her father. "And they're not black. They're a very dark shade of purple. They're Veronica's favorite flower."

"Why am I not surprised?" Polly mumbled.

"Polly, I'm glad you're here," Dr. Winkler said. "I'd like you to meet Captain Grogg. He's an old family friend of the Kreeps."

Captain Grogg smiled at Polly. He had a beard and a gold tooth. An eye patch covered his left eye.

"Captain Grogg will be performing the ceremony," Dr. Winkler explained.

"You're having a *pirate* marry you?" Polly asked.

"Polly!" Dr. Winkler exclaimed. "Grogg is a ship's captain. A very good one, I understand. Don't mind my daughter," he said, turning to Captain Grogg. "She has a very active imagination."

"*Arrrr*," said the captain agreeably. "I been known to imagine a thing or two meself — after a few swigs o' rum, mind you."

Polly looked from Captain Grogg to her dad. *What's the use of explaining?* she thought. She turned and headed for the door.

"Oh, Polly," her dad called after her. "Could you please clean up your room? Grandma Winkler is coming tomorrow. She's going to be staying in there."

"If Grandma's staying in my room, where am I going to sleep?" Polly asked.

"You can sleep in Joy's room," Dr. Winkler

said. "It's just for a couple of nights," he added when she frowned.

Polly sighed and trudged up to her room. When she got there, she shut the door and looked around. Her dad was right. Her room was a mess. But she could deal with that later. She had more important things to do right now.

Polly picked up the phone and dialed Mike's number. She had to tell him about Esme and the cat!

But after a few rings, the answering machine picked up. Polly waited a few minutes and dialed again . . . and again and again. But every time, there was no answer.

At last, Polly gave up. She lay back on her bed and looked up at the ceiling. Polly was more sure than ever that she was right about the Kreeps. But once again, she couldn't prove anything.

✦ Chapter 5 ✦

The next day was the wedding rehearsal. Because the wedding would be small, Dr. Winkler and Veronica had decided to have it in the Kreeps' backyard. So after breakfast on Friday, the Winklers headed across the street to the Kreeps' house.

As they walked, Polly noticed that Petey was reading another book. "What are you memorizing now?" Polly asked. "The encyclopedia?"

"This is a pocket dictionary, for your information," Petey told her.

Polly eyed the fat paperback. "It would

have to be a pretty big pocket for it to fit in," she observed.

As the Winklers climbed the steps of the Kreeps' mansion, they heard a distant rumble, followed by a boom.

Polly's dad looked up at the sky. "I hope that's not a storm coming in," he said. "I'd hate to have rain on our wedding day."

Everyone waited to hear another thunderclap. But the only sound was the frantic buzzing of flies caught in the giant Venus flytraps that grew in the Kreeps' front yard.

"I guess it was nothing," Dr. Winkler said. He reached out and rang the Kreeps' doorbell.

They heard heavy footsteps inside the house. A second later, the door slowly opened.

Polly quickly stepped back.

A giant stood in the doorway, as tall and wide as the door itself. His head was large and square, and his skin was a greenish color. He glared down at the Winklers with bloodshot eyes.

"Yes?" he growled in a voice as deep as a foghorn.

"Hello! We're the Winklers!" Polly's dad said. He grabbed the giant's hand and pumped it up and down. "I'm Dr. Winkler. And this is Joy, Polly, and Petey. You must be Uncle Vlad!"

"No," said the giant. "I am Uncle Frank."

"Oh, well, its great to meet you," said Dr. Winkler.

Uncle Frank nodded his big head in agreement. "Please come in," he said.

He stepped aside to let the Winklers pass. Polly noticed that his hands and face were crisscrossed with scars.

"Sorry if I seem a little cranky," Uncle Frank said when they were all inside. "I arrived late last night. I have not had much sleep."

"You'd better rest up," Dr. Winkler said, slapping him on the arm. "Big day tomorrow."

"Yes, big day tomorrow," Uncle Frank repeated. "Veronica is outside. She's expecting you. If you'll excuse me, I think I'll go lie down."

He lurched off down the hall, his footsteps echoing like falling trees.

Polly pulled her brother and sister aside. "Doesn't Frank remind you of someone?" she hissed.

Petey's brow furrowed thoughtfully. "You mean Dad's cousin Bob?"

"No!" Polly said. "Frankenstein!"

"Oh, Polly. Stop being silly," said Joy.

"I'm not being silly," Polly told her. "He's huge and green! And did you see his scars?"

"That's not very nice," Joy scolded. "How would you like it if people pointed out your freckles?" With a toss of her ponytail, she hurried to catch up with their dad.

Polly sighed. What was it going to take to get her family to see how weird the Kreeps really were?

In back of the Kreeps' house was a great lawn of dead grass. To one side was a pool full of mucky green water. Opposite that, rows of chairs had been set up for the wedding. A tall hedge surrounded the whole backyard. Polly noticed the hedge now looked even worse than it had the day before. It bulged in some places. In others, the branches had been stripped completely bare.

Not a very cheerful place for a wedding, she thought.

Veronica and her three kids were waiting in the yard, holding black umbrellas to shield them from the sun. To Polly, they looked like a clump of deadly mushrooms that had sprouted in the lawn.

"Can you believe this weather we're having?" Dr. Winkler said as the Winklers walked up.

"I know." Veronica sighed, frowning up at the blue sky. "Dreadful, isn't it?"

As they talked, Polly heard a rustle in the hedge near her. *What is that?* she wondered. *Another one of the Kreeps' weird pets?* She leaned down to take a closer look.

"Well," said Dr. Winkler. "Should we get started with the rehearsal?"

"Yes," Veronica said. She looked around. "But where did Esme go? She was here just a minute ago." Putting her hands to her mouth, she called, "Esme! Where are you?"

At that moment, something huge came charging out of the hedge in front of Polly.

41

"Aaaaah!" Polly screamed, stumbling backward.

Esme grinned down at Polly. "Got you," she said.

Polly stood up and brushed herself off, scowling. Magical or not, Esme was turning out to be a real pest.

"Oh, dear. Now we've lost Damon," Veronica said with a sigh. "I swear, keeping track of this family is like trying to herd cats."

"Damon's probably back down in the basement," said Vincent. "He's been working on a new experiment."

"You know, I had a chemistry set when I was a kid, too," Dr. Winkler remarked. "I think it's a terrific hobby."

"Vincent, please go get your brother," said Veronica.

"No way," said Vincent. He glared at his mother from beneath his hood.

"Esme," said Veronica, turning to the little girl. "Will you get Damon, darling?"

Esme shook her head.

"I'll go," Polly said suddenly. Everyone turned to her in surprise. Vincent and Esme looked particularly startled. And, Polly noticed, a little concerned.

Still, she thought, *I can't pass up this chance. I have to see what's in that basement!*

"Thank you, dear," Veronica said. "That's very sweet of you."

"No problem," said Polly, heading toward the house. "Glad to do anything to stop — er, I mean, help with the wedding."

❖ Chapter 6 ❖

Polly stood at the top of the basement steps, staring down into the darkness. The air was cool and damp and smelled like mildew. Polly felt goose bumps on her arms.

Outside, in the warm sunlight, it had seemed like a good idea to explore the basement. But now Polly wasn't so sure. *Anything could be down there,* she thought. *Mice or rats or . . . who knew what else?*

"Don't think about that," Polly told herself. After all, her family was counting on her to find out the truth about the Kreeps — whether they knew it or not.

She reached up and pulled the string to the stair light. There was a soft fizzle, then — *POP!* The lightbulb burned out.

Polly gulped and looked back down the dark stairway. Whatever was down there, she was pretty sure she didn't want to bump into it in the dark.

Just then, she spotted a flashlight next to the door. Before she could think of more reasons to be scared, she grabbed it and headed down the stairs.

When she reached the bottom, she swung the flashlight beam around. She was in a room that looked like a normal cellar. Jars and cans lined the walls. She could hear the *drip, drip, drip* of a leaky pipe.

Suddenly, not far off, she heard a muffled boom. Polly crept toward the sound.

She passed through rooms of boxes, chests, and crates. The Kreeps' basement was much bigger than she'd thought it would be. Polly started to worry that she might never find her way back out.

Just then, she saw an eerie glow. It was coming from a room just ahead. She switched off her flashlight and tiptoed up to the door.

Polly had to cover her mouth to stifle a gasp. The room was filled with strange equipment. Beakers of colorful liquids bubbled over burners and dripped from coiled tubes. Bizarre specimens floated in jars lining the shelves. And in the center of the room, a spiky-haired figure in safety goggles stood rubbing his hands together.

This is no kid's chemistry set, Polly thought. *It's a real mad scientist's lab!*

She jumped as one of the beakers exploded with a bang.

"Miserable molecules!" Damon cursed. "I still haven't got this formula right."

He scuttled over to adjust the burner — and spotted Polly.

Damon chuckled evilly. "Well, well, well," he said. "You've discovered my secret lab."

"Um, hey, Damon," Polly said nervously. "Your mom wants you upstairs. It's time for the, er, wedding rehearsal."

Damon didn't seem to hear. He picked up a flask of red liquid and slowly walked toward her. "And," he went on, "no doubt you've uncovered my sinister plan."

Polly gulped. *Sinister plan?*

"Since you're here," said Damon, "perhaps you'll do me the honor of being my guinea pig — er, guest?"

He held out the flask. Polly looked from the fizzing liquid to Damon's eyes, which seemed to glow behind his safety goggles.

Then she spun on her heel and sprinted away.

"Hey!" cried Damon. "Where are you going?"

But Polly didn't stop. She dashed through the rest of the basement. When she reached the stairs, she took them two at a time.

She burst through the basement door and almost ran into her dad.

"Where have you been, Polly?" Dr. Winkler said. "Everyone is waiting. Where's Damon?"

"Damon has . . . a secret lab . . . in the basement!" Polly cried, gasping for air.

"I know that, honey," said Dr. Winkler. "That's where he does his little science projects."

Polly shook her head. "You don't understand . . . Dad, you have . . . to see it!"

"I'll have plenty of time to see it after the wedding," Dr. Winkler said. "But right now we need to get on with the rehearsal."

At last, Polly managed to catch her breath. She straightened up and exclaimed, "What I'm trying to say, Dad, is that Damon's a mad scientist!"

"Mad?" said Dr. Winkler, his forehead wrinkling. "What does he have to be mad about? Did you two have a fight?"

Just then, Damon appeared in the doorway. "Hello, Dr. Winkler," he said politely. "I was just showing Polly my latest science experiment. I think she found it quite interesting," he added, narrowing his eyes at Polly.

"That's terrific," said Dr. Winkler, patting him on the back. "I'm glad you two are getting along. Let's get this rehearsal going, shall we?"

Polly looked from her dad to Damon. Then, her shoulders slumping, she followed them back outside.

✣ Chapter 7 ✤

"Now that we're all here, we can start the rehearsal," said Veronica.

The two families were gathered in the Kreeps' backyard. Vincent and Damon slouched in the chairs, looking bored out of their minds. Joy, on the other hand, looked like she might burst with excitement.

"So," Veronica went on, "Polly and Joy are the bridesmaids —"

"Yay!" cheered Joy.

"— Damon and Vincent are the groomsmen —"

The boys rolled their eyes.

"— Petey is the ring bearer —"

"That's b-e-a-r-e-r," Petey interrupted, looking up from his dictionary. "Which means someone who carries something. Not b-a-r-e-r, which would mean —"

"Right, Petey," Dr. Winkler said quickly. "You're the ring carrier."

"And Esme is the flower girl," said Veronica. "Do you have your flower petals ready, Esme?"

Esme solemnly nodded and held up her hands. They were cupped tightly together.

"Good," said Veronica. "Now, here's how it will work. When the music starts, Esme will walk down the aisle first, followed by Damon. . . ."

As Veronica talked, Polly suddenly became aware that Esme was watching her. And, more importantly, she was inching closer to her.

Polly leaned over and hissed, "Go bug someone else, Esme!"

Esme gave her a surprised look. Then, without saying a word, she turned and walked over to Petey.

Wow. That was easy, Polly thought.

"Okay," said Veronica. "Does everyone know what they're supposed to do?"

"Got it!" Joy yelled.

Damon and Vincent grunted.

"Got it," said Polly, not really listening. She was busy watching Esme. The little girl was standing right in front of Petey, who still had his nose in his book. Slowly, carefully, Esme opened her cupped hands.

"Petey?" said Dr. Winkler. "Are you paying attention?"

"Huh?" said Petey, looking up. He snapped the dictionary shut — squashing the giant daddy longlegs that Esme had just dropped onto the page.

"Eeee!" Esme squealed.

"What?" said Petey, finally noticing her.

Esme just stared at the dictionary. The spider's long legs could still be seen wiggling from between the pages.

"What's wrong?" Petey asked Esme. "Haven't you ever seen a dictionary before?"

Esme continued to stare at the book. Petey took that to mean "no."

"This is a dictionary," he said, holding up the fat book. "And I am learning to spell everything in it."

Esme's eyes widened. She looked from the book to Petey.

"Of course, I can spell most of it already," Petey went on proudly. "I am a spelling champion, you know."

Esme gave a little gasp.

"Should I spell something for you?" Petey asked, clearly enjoying the attention.

"Noooooooo!" Esme screeched. She clamped her hands over her ears and sprinted away.

Petey turned and looked at Polly. "What got into her?" he asked.

❈ Chapter 8 ❈

As soon as she got home from the rehearsal, Polly called Mike again. To her relief, he answered the phone.

"Where have you been?" Polly cried. "I called you ten times last night!"

"We went to visit my grandparents yesterday," Mike said. "We didn't get home until late."

"You won't believe what's been going on," Polly told him breathlessly. "Esme turned into a cat. Damon has a secret mad scientist's lab in the basement. Oh, and the Kreeps' uncle is Frankenstein!"

"Whoa! Whoa! Slow down!" said Mike. "Esme turned into a *cat*?"

"A little black cat with green eyes," Polly told him.

Polly heard Mike cough — or was it a laugh? She wasn't sure.

Mike cleared his throat. "What makes you think the cat was Esme?" he asked.

Polly explained all about Esme, the cat, and the game of hide-and-seek.

"Let me get this straight," said Mike. "You were playing hide-and-seek with Esme, and you saw her go into the closet."

"Right," said Polly.

"Then, you caught the cat," Mike went on. "And when you looked in the closet again, Esme was gone."

"Exactly!" said Polly.

"But that doesn't prove anything," said Mike. "Esme could have snuck out of the closet when you weren't looking."

"You're forgetting about the necklace," said Polly. "Esme and the cat were wearing the exact same one!"

"So? My grandmother and her poodle wear matching sweaters. That doesn't mean my grandma *is* a poodle," Mike pointed out.

"Are you saying that you don't believe me?" Polly asked.

"No offense, Polly. But it all sounds pretty hard to believe," said Mike.

Polly gripped the phone tightly. She could hardly believe her ears. Mike was her best friend. He was supposed to be on her side.

"Forget it! I never should have called you!" Polly cried. She slammed down the phone.

Just then, her father walked by. "Polly!" he exclaimed when he saw her. "Your room's still a mess! I told you to clean it up

57

yesterday! Get to work right now. Grandma's going to be here any minute."

"Sorry, Dad," Polly said glumly.

As her father strode off down the hall, Polly felt a lump in her throat. It seemed like things were going from bad to worse.

Polly looked around her room. *So what if it's messy?* she thought resentfully. She didn't get what the big deal was. Grandma Winkler was usually pretty understanding about things.

"Grandma!" Polly exclaimed suddenly. Of course! Why hadn't she thought of it before? Her grandmother would understand about the Kreeps. Her grandmother never told Polly she was being silly. In fact, she was always telling her how smart she was! If there was anyone who would believe her, it was Grandma Winkler.

If Grandma knows the truth about the Kreeps, she can tell Dad, Polly thought. He would have to listen to her. After all, she was his mother!

Polly hurriedly started to clean her room. She knew that everything would be okay once her grandmother arrived.

❈ Chapter 9 ❈

Polly stood at the living room window. "When's Grandma getting here?" she asked her father for what felt like the hundredth time.

"I told you, Polly," Dr. Winkler replied. "Her flight was delayed. She might not get in until after you're asleep. Why don't you go to bed now, sweetie. You can see Grandma in the morning."

Polly sighed and turned back to the window. *The morning might be too late,* she thought. "Hurry, Grandma," she whispered to the darkened street.

At that moment, a car pulled into the Winklers' driveway. The door opened, and a small woman with curly, gray hair got out.

"Grandma!" Polly cried. She raced to the front door and was out in the driveway in seconds.

"Boy, am I glad to see you!" Polly said, throwing her arms around her grandmother.

"I'm glad to see you, too, honey," said her grandmother, returning the hug.

"Come on," Polly said. "Let's go inside. I have a *lot* to tell you."

Her grandmother laughed. "Hold your horses," she said. "I still have to pay this nice cab driver."

"I'll take care of that," said Dr. Winkler, coming out of the house. "Hi, Mom. It's great to see you."

"Oh, honey," Grandma Winkler said, giving him a hug, too. "I'm so happy for you. I just knew you would find someone special!"

Dr. Winkler beamed. "I can't wait for you to meet Veronica," he said.

"Well, if she's as wonderful as you say she is, I'm sure you'll be happy together," Grandma Winkler replied.

"All *right*," Polly broke in. "Can you please come inside now, Grandma?"

"Lead the way," said her grandmother.

Inside, Polly fidgeted impatiently while her grandmother hugged Petey and Joy. At last she couldn't wait anymore. "Come on, Grandma. You're staying in my room. I cleaned it up and everything." She grabbed her grandmother by the hand and dragged her up the stairs.

When they were in her room, Polly shut the door. "Grandma," she said seriously, "I have something important to tell you."

Her grandmother sat down on the bed. "I'm all ears," she said.

"Well," said Polly, "it's about the Kreeps. . . ."

Then she told her grandmother everything: about Veronica's strange clothes and spooky hobbies, about Esme and the cat and the room full of masks, about Uncle Vlad and Uncle Frank and Damon's mad scientist lab, and all the other things that made the Kreeps so . . . well, creepy.

Her grandmother listened to everything. She never once interrupted to say "Polly, you're being silly" or "Polly, you're just imagining things."

When Polly was finished, Grandma Winkler asked, "Have you told your dad all this?"

"He doesn't really get it," Polly said. "That's why I need *you* to tell him."

"Me?" asked Grandma Winkler.

"He has to listen to you — you're his mom!" Polly said.

Her grandmother chuckled. "Try telling *him* that," she said.

"But you believe me, don't you, Grandma?" Polly asked.

Grandma Winkler nodded. "I do."

"So why won't you talk to him?" Polly asked.

Grandma Winkler frowned thoughtfully. "I want to show you something," she said.

She got up and left the room. When she came back, she had a book in her hand. "I thought your dad would still have this," she said.

"What is it?" Polly asked.

"It's a book of optical illusions. I gave it to your dad when he was a boy," said

Grandma Winkler. She opened the book and turned to a page. "What do you see?" she asked Polly.

The picture was of an old hag with white hair and a big, warty nose. "An ugly old witch," Polly said.

"Are you sure?"

Polly nodded.

"Look again," said her grandmother.

As Polly looked, the picture seemed to change before her eyes. Now she saw a beautiful woman with her face turned away. The hag's nose became the woman's cheek, her eye became the woman's ear, her hair became the woman's poofy hat.

"Cool!" said Polly. "But I don't see what it has to do with dad."

"When you look at Veronica, you see a witch," said her grandmother. "But when your dad looks at Veronica, he sees a beautiful woman. You both have very different ways of seeing things."

Polly stared at her grandmother in dismay. "Are you saying it's just my imagination?" she asked.

"There's nothing wrong with a having a good imagination," said her grandmother. "In fact, it's wonderful! Without it, you wouldn't be able to see both sides of this illusion. It's funny," she added, tapping the page. "Your father never could see the old hag in this picture."

"I don't care about that stupid picture!" Polly said, jumping to her feet. "I know I'm right about the Kreeps. Why doesn't anyone believe me?"

"Polly —" said her grandmother.

But Polly wasn't listening anymore. Turning on her heel, she ran out of the room.

❧ Chapter 10 ❧

That night, Polly lay awake in Joy's double bed. She stared at the ceiling, turning things over in her mind.

She had been so certain that there was something . . . *supernatural* about the Kreeps. But nobody believed her. Not her dad or her brother or her sister. Not her grandmother. Not even her best friend.

Was it possible they were all right, and she was wrong?

"But I *saw* it," Polly whispered to herself. She couldn't have imagined everything, could she?

Polly turned onto her side. The clock on

Joy's nightstand read 2:07. In just a few more hours, the Kreeps were going to be her family.

Whap! Suddenly, something punched her in the back of the head.

"Ow!" Polly cried. She sat up. Joy was lying on her back in the bed, her arms straight out at her sides. Both of her hands were curled into fists.

"What did you do that for?" Polly asked, rubbing her head.

"Go, Bulldogs!" Joy murmured.

Polly looked closer. Her sister's eyes were closed. "You've got to be kidding me," Polly grumbled. Joy was cheerleading in her sleep!

Joy gave a soft snore and rolled over. Polly lay back down and closed her eyes. A second later, Joy kicked her in the shin.

"Ouch! Stop it!" Polly hissed.

"Hooray!" Joy muttered.

Polly hopped out of bed. At this rate, she would be black and blue by morning! She grabbed her pillow and her bathrobe and headed off to find another place to sleep.

In the living room, Polly flopped down on the couch. The window was cracked open, and a cool breeze blew in. From where she was sitting, Polly could see the Kreeps' big, wooden house. A full moon rose behind it.

Just then, she heard a noise out in the street: *Snick-snick-snick-snick.*

It sounded like wheels on pavement. Polly pressed her nose to the glass, trying to see what was making it.

A hooded figure was gliding down the street. *That looks like Vincent,* Polly thought. He was riding his skateboard. But what was he doing out so late?

Vincent crossed the street, going fast. When he reached the sidewalk, he hopped the curb. But he didn't come down. His skateboard just kept rising in the air.

"Oh, my gosh!" Polly shrieked.

"Polly?" said a voice behind her.

The living room lights flicked on. Polly blinked in the sudden brightness. Her dad was standing in the doorway, squinting sleepily.

"What are you doing?" he said.

"Dad!" Polly exclaimed. "I just saw Vincent flying on his skateboard!"

"Vincent's out riding his skateboard?" Dr. Winkler asked. "At this hour?"

"Not riding, *flying*. Look!" She turned back to the window. But all she could see was her own reflection.

"Oh, the lights!" Polly cried.

She hurried over and flipped them off.

Together, they looked out the window. The street was as still and quiet as a tomb.

"He was out there, Dad," Polly said. "I swear. I —"

Dr. Winkler cleared his throat. "It's okay, Polly," he said. "I know what's going on."

She looked at him in surprise. "You do?"

Dr. Winkler nodded. "It's perfectly natural to be worried, honey," he said, putting an arm around her. "To be honest with you, I'm a little nervous, too."

"You are?" Polly asked.

"Sure," said Dr. Winker. "But even though things might seem strange at first, I think once we get used to them, we can all be happy together."

Polly could hardly believe what she was hearing. "So you know about Esme and the cat? And Uncle Vlad's coffin? And the

71

rattlesnake? And you're *okay* with it?" she asked in amazement.

"Cat . . . coffin . . . rattlesnake? What are you talking about?" Dr. Winkler looked utterly perplexed. "Sweetie, I was talking about being a family!"

"Oh." Disappointment choked Polly's throat. Her dad didn't understand after all.

Dr. Winkler brushed Polly's bangs out of her eyes. "Promise me you'll at least try to keep an open mind about Veronica and her kids," he said.

Polly looked out the window again. The street was empty. Vincent was long gone. *But maybe he was never there,* Polly thought. *Maybe I really am imagining everything.*

Maybe the best thing to do was to try to see things the way her dad saw them.

Polly turned back from the window. "Okay," she said. "I promise."

❈ Chapter 11 ❈

Saturday morning, Polly stood in the Kreeps' backyard, marveling at the sight. Overnight, the place had been transformed. Shiny black ribbons hung from the trees, stirring ever so slightly in the warm breeze. Bouquets of black calla lilies lined the aisle. A wedding cake covered with black licorice roses rested on a table in the corner of the yard. The hedges, too, had finally taken shape. Vincent and Damon had trimmed them into monsters with gaping jaws and bulging eyes. A few of them held balloons in their twiggy claws, courtesy of Joy.

Polly had to admit, it was all impressive — in a Halloweenish sort of way.

Polly looked down at her bridesmaid dress, which had also been transformed. The bell-shaped sleeves were gone, replaced by pretty ribbon straps. The waist fit perfectly now. *Veronica did work some magic on it,* Polly thought.

But it wasn't really magic, she reminded herself. After all, lots of people could sew.

Veronica was by the garden gate, greeting the guests as they came in. She was wearing a long, red wedding gown, elbow-length gloves, and a matching bloodred veil.

"No," Polly said quietly to herself, shaking her head. "Not *blood*red. Just red. Plain old red."

Ever since her conversation with her dad, Polly had been practicing seeing things the way the rest of her family saw them. For example, that was not Bigfoot shaking hands with Veronica, she told herself. It was just a tall, hairy man with skateboard-sized feet. The squat man sitting next to Uncle Frank was not a troll, he was just a short guy with very large ears. And that woman over by the cauldron of punch was not a cannibal queen, she was just a regular person with a bone in her nose.

"And it's not a cauldron," Polly reminded herself. "It's just a big, black punch bowl."

Just then, Polly spotted a familiar figure in the crowd of guests. Mike came hustling over to her.

"I've been trying to call your house all morning!" he said. He was huffing and puffing, as if he'd run the whole way there.

"I guess no one heard the phone," Polly

said. "We were all getting ready for the wedding."

"Listen, Polly," Mike said, lowering his voice, "last night —"

"I've been thinking about last night, too," Polly interrupted. "All that stuff I told you about the Kreeps really was crazy."

Mike's eyes widened. "But —"

"I've just been nervous about the wedding," Polly went on. "So I've been imagining things that aren't really there."

"But —"

"You were right all along, Mike," Polly finished. "I'm sorry I yelled at you."

"No, *you* were right," Mike said. "That's what I've been trying to tell you. Late last night, I woke up and looked out the window. I swear I saw Vincent — on a flying skateboard!"

Polly gasped. "You saw him, too?"

"It was the coolest thing I'd ever seen," Mike said, nodding. "So I ran and got my dad's digital camera — he has a special lens for nighttime — and I got this picture!"

Mike held up a photo that he'd printed from his computer. The picture was a little blurry, but Polly could just make out Vincent soaring through the air. She could see rooftops in the background.

"Mike!" Polly cried, grabbing the picture. "You're a genius! I have to show this to my dad!"

Polly looked around. Suddenly, she realized all the guests were seated. The wedding was about to start!

"Come on, Mike. We're almost out of time!" she exclaimed.

Dr. Winkler was standing by the wedding cake, straightening his cuff links. Polly and Mike raced over to him.

"There you are, Polly," Dr. Winkler said. "Ready to go?"

"Look, Dad!" said Polly, shoving the picture under his nose. "It's a picture of Vincent. And he's flying, just like I told you!"

Dr. Winkler glanced at the picture and frowned. "Hmm. He is catching some big air. I should talk to him about wearing a helmet."

Just then, he noticed Mike. "Shouldn't you go sit down, Mike?" he said. "The wedding is about to start."

"But . . . but . . . aren't you going to stop the wedding?" Polly asked her dad.

Dr. Winkler looked startled. "Stop the wedding? Why, for goodness' sake?"

At that moment, Veronica came hurrying toward them. She was saying something. But for a second, Polly couldn't understand what.

Then she heard the words loud and clear.

"Stop!" Veronica was saying. "Stop the wedding! Stop the music! Esmerelda is missing!"

❊ Chapter 12 ❊

E sme!" Polly yelled. "Esme, where are you?"

The only answer was the chirping of cicadas. In the distance, Polly could hear other people calling Esme's name. Everyone from the wedding had split up to look for her.

Polly wondered what kind of crazy trick Esme was pulling now. But she couldn't help feeling a little worried, too. *What if something really bad happened?* she thought.

Polly was about to turn down another

block, when Vincent came running up to her. "Mom sent me to find you," he said. "We found Esme. Come on!"

Polly ran with him back to the Kreeps' house. When they got there, everyone was in the backyard. They were standing around an enormous maple tree, staring up at the branches. Polly could see Esme's small, white face hidden among the leaves.

"I just don't understand how a five-year-old got all the way up there!" Dr. Winkler was exclaiming. "It's impossible. Just impossible!"

Polly could only think of one way Esme could have gotten so high up. She had climbed — like a cat!

Veronica was standing on a tall ladder, talking to the little girl. But a moment later she climbed down — alone. "She won't come down," Veronica told them.

"But what's she doing up there?" Dr. Winkler asked. "She could fall and get hurt!"

"I know." Veronica wrung her hands worriedly. Suddenly she turned to Polly and asked, "Will you talk to her?"

"Me?" Polly exclaimed.

"She might listen to you," said Veronica. "She looks up to you, you know."

"She does?"

Veronica nodded. "Haven't you ever noticed how she's always following you around?"

Polly was astonished. Could that be why Esme was always playing tricks on her? Was it just that she'd wanted Polly's attention?

Polly looked back up in the tree. She could see Esme's big, green eyes peering down at them.

"All right," she said. "I'll go."

"Please be careful," Veronica said. Polly nodded.

Uncle Frank held the ladder steady while Polly started to climb. She climbed all the way up, until she was level with Esme.

"Hey, Esme. What are you doing?" she asked.

"Hiding," said the little girl.

"Well, guess what. I found you this time," said Polly. "So now you have to come down."

Esme shook her head.

"Come on," said Polly. "I'll help you."

"I don't want to," said Esme.

Polly was starting to get annoyed. She was risking her neck for this weird little kid! "Why not?" she snapped.

Esme blinked. She looked like she might cry. Suddenly, Polly realized that Esme really was frightened. "What are you scared of?" Polly asked, more gently.

"Joy," said Esme.

"My sister?!" Polly exclaimed. She almost laughed. "What's so scary about her?"

"She has a scary smile," Esme said. "And Petey's scary too. He almost put a spell on me!"

"Esme, that's sill —" Polly broke off. She had been about to say it was silly. But Esme didn't think it was silly, Polly realized. She really was scared of Petey and Joy.

And why wouldn't she be? Polly thought. After all, Polly thought Esme's family was totally weird. Why wouldn't Esme think her family was weird, too?

Polly looked down at the ground. Her dad and Veronica had their arms around each other, looking up into the tree. Right at that moment, Veronica didn't look at all like a witch, Polly thought. She just looked like a mom who was worried about her kid.

Polly was starting to think maybe there had been something to what Grandma Winkler said. There were different ways of looking at things — and maybe both could be right. Maybe Veronica could be a witch and also be a good mom. Maybe Esme could be spooky and magical and still be a little girl who needed a big sister.

Maybe the Kreeps could be weird and still be Polly's family.

"You know what, Esme?" she said. "Joy and Petey are pretty weird. But I think you'll be okay," she said. "In fact, I'll make sure of it."

"You will?" said Esme.

Polly nodded. "Will you come down now?" she asked.

Esme hesitated. "All right," she said at last.

Carefully, Polly helped Esme down the ladder. When they got to the bottom, Dr. Winkler and Veronica both hugged them.

"Thank you, Polly," said Veronica. "I was so worried."

"Me, too," Polly said. "But I think it'll be okay."

"I still don't understand how Esme got all the way up there!" Dr. Winkler said, shaking his head.

Polly smiled. "You'd never believe me if I told you," she said.

✦ Chapter 13 ✦

Veronica, do ye take this landlubber to be yer lawfully wedded husband?" asked Captain Grogg.

Veronica smiled. "I do."

"And, Wally, do ye take this lass to be yer lawfully wedded wife?" Captain Grogg asked.

"I do," said Dr. Winkler, grinning.

"*Arrrrr*," said Captain Grogg. "Then, by the blasted powers in me, I now pronounce ye husband and wife. Ye may kiss her, matey!" he added, slapping Dr. Winkler on the back.

Dr. Winkler and Veronica leaned in to kiss, and everyone burst into applause. Joy waved her bouquet like a pom-pom, shouting, "Go, Dad! Go, Veronica!"

Captain Grogg wiped a tear from his one good eye. "Weddings always make me blubber," he sniffled.

Polly watched her father and her new mother walk back down the aisle. She felt sad and happy all at once.

Esme tugged Polly's hand. "So now we're sisters?" she asked.

"That's right," Polly told her.

"And we share things?" Esme asked.

"Some things," said Polly.

"Then, I'll share Bubbles with you!" Esme offered gallantly. Before Polly could say anything, she drew out the spider from her pocket and placed it on Polly's hand.

"Aaah!" Polly cried.

"Don't move too fast," Esme warned her. "It makes her cranky."

Polly froze.

"Well, see you later," said Esme. She skipped away.

Polly whimpered as the spider started to crawl up her arm.

As the crowd broke up, Mike walked over to her. "Did you know there's a bug on you?" he asked.

"Very funny," said Polly. "Please get it off."

Mike let the huge spider crawl onto his hand. "You know, tarantulas are usually harmless. You should try holding her. I bet you'll get used to it pretty quickly," he said.

"One thing at a time," said Polly. "First, I have to get used to having Esme as a sister."

"So, are you okay?" Mike asked. "About the Kreeps being your family, I mean."

Polly looked over at her dad and Veronica. Joy, Petey, Vincent, Damon, and Esme were all gathered around them, posing for a picture.

"Come on, Polly!" Veronica called, waving to her. "We need you!"

"You know what?" Polly said to Mike. "I think I am."

The last dregs of sunlight were draining from the sky by the time they sat down for dinner. A long banquet table had been set up in the Kreeps' backyard for the wedding feast. Candles flickered in huge candelabras, casting a cozy glow over everything.

Once everyone was seated, Dr. Winkler tapped his glass with a spoon. "May I have your attention?" he said. "Let me begin by saying how happy I am that you . . ."

His words dwindled away. He was staring at something just beyond the table. Everyone turned to see what he was looking at.

A tall, gaunt figure was approaching. As it stepped into the light, Polly saw it was a man. But what a strange man! His skin was as white as chalk. His dark eyes were sunken in his face. He was dressed in a black silk suit with an elegant red scarf wrapped around his neck. Polly noticed his fingernails were extremely long.

"Uncle Vlad!" cried Veronica, rising to her feet.

"*That's* Uncle Vlad? He really does look like a vampire," Mike whispered to Polly.

"Please, don't get up," Uncle Vlad said to Veronica. "I'm sorry to have missed the ceremony. I haven't been feeling well. I'm afraid the sunny climate here doesn't agree with me."

"Well, we're just glad you made it," said Dr. Winkler kindly, though he looked slightly unnerved by the strange visitor.

"I'd like to propose a toast," said Uncle Vlad.

He picked up a glass from the table. It was filled with dark, red liquid. Uncle Vlad raised it high and said, "To the happy couple. Long may you live . . ."

"To the couple!" Everyone reached for their glasses.

"*Tut!*" Uncle Vlad scolded. "I am not done yet." He lifted his glass again. "And to family. May you always be there for one another. For, as we all know, blood is thicker than water."

"To family!" everyone cried, raising their glasses.

Polly looked around. All the glasses were filled with bubbling red liquid. Suddenly, she noticed Damon. He was grinning and rubbing his hands together gleefully.

Damon's sinister plan! Polly thought with a gasp. "No!" she cried out to everyone. "Don't drink it! It's —"

Too late! Everyone downed the liquid.

"Oh, no!" Polly whispered.

A queasy look passed across Uncle Vlad's face. In fact, everyone was looking a little ill.

Then, all at once, their mouths opened and —*B U R P!*

Everyone burped at once. The combined force of the blast was so great it made the dishes rattle!

Damon threw back his head, laughing

maniacally. "It worked!" he screeched. "My super-burp strawberry soda is a success!"

Strawberry soda? Polly thought, her jaw dropping. *That was Damon's sinister plan?*

Polly couldn't help it. She started to laugh. Pretty soon everyone else was laughing, too.

"Your family is crazy, Polly," Mike whispered.

Polly smiled. "You haven't seen anything yet," she said.

"Well, I don't know about anyone else, but I'm hungry!" Dr. Winkler boomed jovially. "Let's eat!"

The silver platters on the table were uncovered and dinner was dished out.

As Dr. Winkler stuffed a bite into his mouth, his eyes widened in surprise. "This tastes like chicken!" he exclaimed. "I thought we ordered steak!"

Polly met Veronica's eyes. Veronica winked at her, and Polly smiled back. Then she turned to her dad and said, "Forget the steak, Dad. A party just isn't a party without a roasted rattlesnake."

Polly's adventures with
the Kreeps continue in

Meet the Kreeps

The Nanny
Nightmare

Turn the page for a sneak
peek . . . if you dare!

❊ The Nanny Nightmare ❊

W hat was that?" Polly Winkler said with a gasp.

She sat up in bed. It was the middle of the night, and her room was dark. Just a thin sliver of moonlight shone between the curtains on her window.

Polly stared into the darkness, her eyes round. Out in the hallway, something was moving. She held her breath and listened.

Scratch. Scratch. Scratch. Scratch.

It was a steady scrabbling sound. *Like a dog trying to get in*, Polly thought.

She froze, hugging the bedcovers to her

chest. She wondered if she should wake her dad. But his room was down a long, dark, cobwebby hallway. Polly didn't like to go there if she could help it.

This was not the first time she had woken to weird sounds in the night. It had only been a few days since she'd moved into her stepfamily's mansion, but Polly had hardly slept a wink since. The Kreeps' gloomy house, so dark and silent by day, seemed to come alive at night. Mice skittered behind the walls. Bats fluttered against the windows. And there were other noises, too — strange creaks and groans that Polly couldn't explain.

Still, she had never heard a sound like this.

Scratch. Scratch. Scratch.

"Vincent?" Polly said softly, thinking it might be her oldest stepbrother. He sometimes stayed out riding his skateboard long past midnight. Maybe he had gotten locked out.

But Vincent would have a key, Polly thought. *And if he didn't, he would knock.* Besides, this sounded like it was coming from inside the house.

Polly pushed back the covers and climbed out of bed. Feeling her way through the dark room, she tiptoed to the door. She crouched down and put her ear to the keyhole.

Silence.

She stayed a moment longer, listening. All she could hear was the loud pounding of her own heart. Slowly, carefully, she inched the door open.

The hallway was empty.

Polly exhaled. She opened the door all the way and stepped into the hall.

Moonlight shone through a high round window. It bathed the hallway in silvery light. The rug Polly was standing on had a pattern of twisting vines. In the weird light, they seemed to writhe like snakes.

Polly quickly stepped off the rug. She shivered and wrapped her arms around herself. *I should just go back to bed,* she thought. The house was spooky enough by day. She didn't need to be poking around at night.

Thump!

The sound almost scared her out of her skin. She spun around. It had come from the door at the end of the hall, she realized. Something was pounding against it.

Just then, Polly noticed the door to her stepsister's room was open. She looked in and saw that the bed was empty.

It's just Esme, Polly thought, sighing with relief. *She must have gotten up to use the bathroom. Maybe she accidentally locked herself in.* It wouldn't have been the first time that it happened. Esme was only five years old, after all.

Polly went over to the door. She knocked softly. "Esme?" she murmured. "Are you okay in there?"

There was no answer. Polly heard a wet, snuffling sound on the other side of the door.

"Esme?" she said again. She reached for the doorknob.

But the door suddenly flew open. A dark shape loomed over Polly. She caught a glimpse of glowing red eyes, before two rough, hairy hands grabbed her and dragged her inside.

Polly screamed.

If you dare to

Meet the Kreeps

check out the rest of the
spooky series!

Turn the page to learn more . . .
if you have the nerve . . .

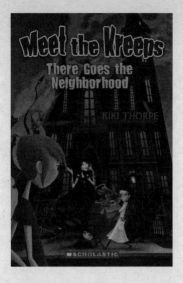

Meet the Kreeps #1: There Goes the Neighborhood

Polly Winkler is not excited to meet her new neighbors, the Kreeps. The family is as weird as their name — and as strange as the spooky, possibly haunted, house they're moving into. They might be next door, but Polly is determined to keep the Kreeps out of her life.

But Polly's dad actually likes the new neighbors, especially beautiful (but odd!) Veronica. Can Polly save her normal family from the creepy Kreeps?

Meet the Kreeps #3:
The Nanny Nightmare

When Polly's dad and his new wife, Veronica
Kreep, go on their honeymoon, Polly, Joy, and
Petey Winkler are stuck alone with their weird
new step-siblings, the Kreep kids, living in the
Kreeps' spooky old mansion. Things get even
worse when their sinister sitter, Ms. Pearl, shows
up. Even sunny Joy and oblivious Petey have to
admit that Polly might be right: Something weird
is going on in the Kreep mansion! The kids have
to find a way to get rid of Ms. Pearl. And they
just might need the Kreeps' help to do it.